NHL MASCOTS & Friends

WRITTEN BY
Holly Preston

ILLUSTRATED BY
James Hearne

Always Books Ltd.

NHL Mascots & Friends

Text and illustrations © 2014 Always Books, Ltd.

Manufactured by Friesens Corporation in Altona, MB, Canada
January 2017
Job # 229683

Library and Archives Canada Cataloguing in Publication

Preston, Holly, author
NHL mascots & friends / written by Holly Preston ; illustrated by James Hearne.

ISBN 978-0-9938974-2-9 (pbk.)

I. Hearne, James, 1972-, illustrator II. Title. III. Title: NHL
mascots and friends.

PS8631.R467N45 2015   jC813'.6   C2014-907075-6

Layout by Heather Nickel

FSC
www.fsc.org
MIX
Paper from
responsible sources
FSC® C016245

Always Books Ltd.

AFANFORLIFE.COM

AUTOGRAPHS

Yippee and hooray!
You won't want it to end.

Youppi! has a party for all his friends.
You're invited to attend!

Hunter's a lynx.
He just loves hockey hijinks.

Victor E. Green has come to play from an alien place far away.

Wild Wing makes an entrance.
You'll know he's arrived.

Quack!
Quack!

Tommy Hawk is so proud
of his team.

It looks like
you are, too!

BANG!

BANG!

BANG!

Howler lets everyone know his team is ready to score.

Sabretooth sees the game like nobody else.

Would upside-down hockey be so hard to play?

Iceburgh is the coolest
dancing penguin on Earth.

Lightning strikes when
ThunderBug steps on the ice.

Stormy seems calm
but watch out for
what's brewing!

Stanley C. Panther is on the prowl for the Cup.

Then you see Stinger and wonder what's up?

Sparky loves to play hockey.
Just look and see why!

Nordy is unique.

His style is so wild!

Sparky loves to play hockey.
Just look and see why!

Spectacular Slapshot soars
above all the rest.

★ ★ ★
WASHINGTON
capitals

S.J. Sharkie is the hardest working fish in the NHL. That makes him so hungry!

Oh, what is there to eat?

Nordy is unique.

His style is so wild!

N.J. Devil is a devilish guy,
but he's friendly to fans
who want to high five!

The Moose takes control—
he likes to fly high!

Gnash is a prankster—
(I hope you like pie).

Fin has a whale of a time. The Canucks are his team.

Come cheer them on (but don't lose your head!)

Carlton gives bear hugs
when it's time for bed.

... they never hibernate when there's a game to be played.

Blades and Louie know the "bear" facts of hockey...

Harvey is the most hilarious hound...

... his tongue just gets twisted around and around!

Bernie is so brave, his team won't get snowed under.

Bailey boldly announces he is "King of the rink."

Spartacat roars, "No, that's me!"

Al the Octopus
is amazing.

How *does* he keep his
tentacles untangled?

My Special Mascot Friend is

_____

AUTOGRAPHS

ABOUT THE AUTHOR
Holly Preston

Holly Preston is a journalist who worked for CTV and CBC. She grew up watching NHL hockey with her brother and father. Now she creates children's picture books for professional sports teams. She hopes young NHL fans will enjoy having a book that celebrates the mascot of their home team.

ABOUT THE ILLUSTRATOR
James Hearne

Born in London England, James began his art career at the tender age of eight, selling drawings to guests at his grandparents' hotel. He continues to sell his whimsical illustrations around the globe as a full-time illustrator and full-time hockey fan.